Choctaw Capitol at Tushkahoma, Oklahoma

LIMITED EDITION # _____ **of 1,000**

1903 - 1972
Author - Mary M. Frye

Translator - Henry J.
Willis

Illustrator - Norma
Howard

Push and Indian Time

is dedicated to

Chief Gregory E. Pyle
&
Assistant Chief Mike Bailey

Choctaw Nation Council

Charley Jones
Mike Amos
Kenny Bryant
Delton Cox
Charlotte Jackson
Randle Durant
Jack Austin
Perry Thompson
Ted Dosh
E.J. Johnson
Bob Pate
James Frazier

Series of five:

The Pashofa Pole
Push and Indian Time
The Stomachache Tree
The Boy Who Almost Lost His Name
Choctaw Jacks

A special thanks to H.V. Chapman & Sons, Book Binders of Abilene, Texas,
for the beautiful work they have contributed to the Choctaw Nation Children's books.

Choctaw Nation
Education Dept.
Drawer 1210
Durant, Oklahoma 74702
ISBN: 0-9710250-3-7

Push and Indian Time

(A Children's Book)

Author – Mary M. Frye

Illustrator – Norma Howard

Translator – Henry J. Willis

Editor in chief – Joy Culbreath

Editor – Marcia Haag

Push Anonti Hattak Vpi Humma Hvshi Kanvlli

Selena anonti Push itatuklot iholita okissa itonvchi ma
Selena yvt apishia itikba pit balilit isht ia tok. Push vt halvllit
falamichi tok. "Ish yvmmohmachih keyo!" Nukoa hosh afalvpat
anumpuli tok. Nashuka itohlakvbi yvt hummvt isht ia tok.
Nishkin lusa yvt tohpohlohlit kania tok.

Selena yvt okchihlunlit pisa tok. "Koh, chipesa okpulo,
Push. Peh nana achi sabvnna . . . ."

"Chishnakosh Ipokni ya imanoli chi bvnna tuk. Ikhana li.
Anakosh yvmmohmi li tuk. Anakosh imanoli lachi."

Selena yvt okchihlunlit pisa moma tok. Pisa ka nukoa
fehna tok. Yvmmvt nakfish ikyimmo choyohmi tok, peh himo
afvmmi hvnnali atuk, afvmmi tuklo alotowa hosh iklauecho tok.
"Ome," achi mvt, "yohmi kia holhtina pokkoli hotina lachi?
Chik ishtio kisha hokma, anakosh imanoli lachi."

1

Ipokni yᵥt imapishia itikba, abinili faiohlichi okchamali ombinnilit, tobi hakshish hl̲i̲fi hosh bininli tok. Push ᵥt tobi aiimma okla isht anumpula hetuk ahni tok. Okchanki moma na̲ ibbᵥk alota achᵥffa ishi cha ᵥpa kᵥt imachukma tok. Yohmi kia Ipokni yᵥt tobi pisa keyu tok. Ibbak itohl̲a̲kᵥbi yᵥt tobi hakshish hl̲i̲fi t̲a̲kla kᵥt apissalit pisa tok.

"Ʋla, sᵥlahat hᵥsh ittᵥlachi," achi tuk.

Push ᵥt itipᵥtalhpo pisa tukᵥt achunnanchit ᵥba chakali tok. Nishkin ᵥt ᵥba iat nafohka tikba takali anonti ibbak ont aiahlichi tok. Mihmᵥt, Selena haklo tok, "achᵥffa, tuklo, tuchina...."

Inoti itiksilechi cha Ipokni ḏinishkin apissalit pisa tok. Fiopa achᴠffalit miha tok, "Pehlichi apela pit sachᴠffichi tok."

"Ithanali," Ipokni yᴠt achi tok. Ibbᴠk ato toksahanli kia nashuka ᴠto anumpulit mahaya chi ka hoyo . . .tok.

"Afoha ᴠlhpisa ya ont iachit sᴠlaha .... li tuk. Nittak tuchina ka .... tabokoli ont ia hituchinachit ittiakaiyachi li tuk."

"Chitolit anumpuli, Push, itipatalhpo ano ish pisa na," achi tok.

"Yohmi kᴠt—nittak ᴠmmona kano, Chimi ittibi li tuk. Nukoat il ittibi tuk keyu. Yᴠmmakosh akana moma inshahli. Peh e yokopa he keyu tuk."

"Ohoyo himmita Sims ato nanta ho achi tuk?" Yohmachi ka, Selena yᴠt atᴠklamᴠt anumpuli tok."

"Ittatuklochit pim anumpuli tuk," achi tok.

"Mikma atukla kano?" Ipokni yᴠt ponaklo tok.

"Pilashash, yᴠmma atukla ka, inla ibayat chukoa li naha tuk. Yohmi kia na shali yᴠt ant yokopa ka pisa li tuk. Humma atuk. Chito kᴠt yᴠmmafoka ak piso chatuk osh pisali tok. Kanihmi kia, ont pisa sabᴠnna tuk."

"Atuk o anonti ish salaha tuk." Selena yᴠt anumpa tahpᴠla naha tok.

Habli bᴠnna tok. Yohmi kia, nan ataklᴠma ibachukoat ᴠlhtaha tok. Mihma Ipokni ḏinashuka yᴠt hoyo moma tok.

3

"Pilashash ohoyo himmita Sims *v*t falayachi hosh anumpuli tuk. Anak fehna *v*m anumpuli tuk."

Ipokni y*v*t chitolit fiopa tok "Yohmi kia chik haklo ketuk amahowa. Keyukm*v*t nahullo imanumpa chik imithano."

Push *v*t komota chi̱ tok. I̱nashuka y*v*t humma kania tok. Ishki anonti i̱ki y*v*t atoksali ya̱ falamat italachik mak a hetuk ahni tok. Mahli h*v*t apishia mahlichit akka sa pila maka hetuk ahni tok.

Polanka achi tuk "H*v*klo li tuk, yohmi kia amihaksi tuk. Himak nitt*v*k, Sesal Kle *v*t am uskulushi *v*m eshi ma......"

"Koh, Push *v*lla nakni y*v*mm*v*t chitoh. Y*v*mm*v*t ont isht tahlapi aiitapiha pisa." Selena y*v*t achi tok.

"Y*v*mm*v*t chito k*v*t a̱shahlih. Yohmi kia balili palhki k*v*t i̱shahlichi la hinla. Am oskulushi pit yichiffit balili li tuk. Balihinlili tuk. Balilit hopakichili tukosh . . . . anonti s*v*lahat ona li tuk."

Ahchibat taha ma̱ Ipokni y*v*t ponaklo tok. "Atuk o̱ ohoyo himmita Sims *v*t pilechi apela chishtia tuk o̱?"

"Keyu sashtia tuk keyu. Holisso pisa *v*t tishili hako̱ pit sach*v*ffichi tuk."

"Hattak Klam *v*t okpulo tuk o̱? Chi fama tuk o̱." Selena y*v*t yimmitat kania hosh ponaklo tok.

Push *v*t ibbak katanlichit bonulli tok. Il*v*pp*v*t ont lusho̱ma hokmalusho̱ma chi̱ yoba hokma—Selena ya̱ mahl*v*llit kanchi achi̱. Himonasi ano ill*v*pp*v*k illa ho̱ achi tok, "Keyu, okpulo tuk keyu. Micha safama tuk keyu."

4

"Peh anumpuli tuk. Kanima ak<u>o</u> e m<u>a</u>ya chi tukm_vt mak<u>o</u> e m<u>a</u>ya hinla tuk. Atuk <u>o</u> imabachi anonti k_vna inla aiena k_vt pi yoshoba keyu k<u>a</u> okla ikhana hinla tuk."

Ipokni y_vt yukpa naha tok. 'Hattak _vpi humma h_vshi kan_vlli ish iakaiya h<u>o</u>?' Achit chi ponaklo h<u>a</u>?"

"Y_vmm_vt nanta?" Push anonti Selena y_vt ponaklo tok.

"Himonnah m<u>a</u>, Chahta—hattak _vpi humma moma k_vt— h_vshi kan_vlli ont ai_vlhpesa hokma aiyokohmichi tok. H_vshi kan_vllit ont ai_vlhpesa hokma hattak _vt anumpuli chatuk; hattak inla hosh anumpolach<u>i</u> ai_vlhpisa ano atakl_vmma hekeyu tok."

"Nan _vni y_vt nuna _vlhpesakmat _vlmo tok— cheki keyuk m_vt hopaki at_vpa keyu. Himak nittak _vno, nan _vni y_vt nuna keyu hokm<u>a</u> osapa inla ilaishih. H_vshi ai_vlhpesa keyu mak<u>o</u> pim<u>a</u>sha hinla. Atuk <u>o</u> himak _vno, nana y_vt ont ai_vlhpesa mak<u>o</u> e yohmi keyu amba h_vshi kan_vlli anoli ako il iakaya."

5

Ipokni yʌt Push bilikachit isht ʌla mʌt ibbak hoklit ishi tok. "Nan inlachi moma kʌt aiokpuloka keyu. Ohoyo himmita Sims ʌt tʌli ola iakaiya chi tukʌt imihaksik mano? Yohmi kʌt ohoyo himmita Sims ʌt ilap ahnit imaiʌlhtaha akosh hachichukka hʌsh ia chi ka hachimissak mano? Hʌshi kanʌlli tuchina iklʌnnakma chihoyoli na hachik haiako hokma nanokpulo hachi ataklʌmma tuk ahnit samahlʌla hinla."

"Himak nittak a hattak ʌpi humma moma kʌt ilap salaha kʌt isht yopula. 'Hattak ʌpi humma hʌshi kanʌlli iakaiyah osh yohmi ho?' kʌnat ponaklo pulla chi aiahli."

"Push chohmi?" Selena yʌt ponaklo tok.

Himak hikiat ia kano Push a chohma achi keyu. Yʌmmʌt aiahli. Himak ʌno hattak ʌpi humma hʌshi kanʌlli yʌt ʌmohma hekeyu. Yohmi mʌt, Push isholush shafa ahiket iat panshi lusa ont aiahli achukmalit pisa tok. "Push, chi sa na yukpali chohmi."

"I na yukpali?" Selena yʌt nukoat kashkachit anumpuli bilia tok. "Anakosh pehlichi apela itikba iali tukmano. . . . ."

"Issa, Selena. Nana akaniohmi tuk ano isht sa na yukpali ahli keyu. Amba ilap bʌnno hosh Hattak Klam i nan isht atta aboha ia tuk ako isht sa nayukpa."

"Ak...akio naha tuk." Push ʌt kanihmi kia imanoli tok. "Imokhisa hetuchina ona li kia kucha pit balili li tuk. Atuk kia falamʌt ona li tuk. Ont hikia li tuk. Ahmʌt komohlichi li tuk."

"Yohmi kia ish ia tuk." Ipokni yʌt ikhʌnanchi tok. "Atukosh Chahta ahli chia."

"Kʌtihmi ho?" Push ʌt Selena ya imaiyachit ponaklo tok.

6

"Yohmi ka Chahta yʋt ilap i̱ yakni balilichi momah ma̱, achʋffa aiyukali kʋt isikkopalachi̱kma̱ . . . ilap bano hosh——haiaka billia tuk. Aiokpulo kaniohmit aiisht ilbʋsha chi̱ makosh. Okla wak hu̱kupa tukmʋt, fʋma tok. Kʋna ʋbi tukmʋt kanimi kia okla nʋhla tok."

"Nanʋlhtoka yʋt aboha kʋllo apitta keyu tok o̱?" Push ʋt ponaklo tok.

"Aboha kʋllo ʋt iksho tok. Mikmʋt nanʋlhtoka yʋt iksho tok. Issuba Ombinili Tʋshka yʋt yakni apakfoyupat nan ataklama lohmachit tok. Yʋmma ithanali moma."

Push micha Selena yʋt chulusat haklo bʋnna moma tok.

"Nahla chi hosh falamʋt ʋla hokma̱, ikishi akanima ho̱ nakni yʋt aiissachi ka̱ hlʋfa humma takalichi tok." Kanihmikma̱, ilap akinli hosh ikishi ya̱ hlʋfa humma takalichi tok.

"Yʋmmʋt . . . . yʋmmʋt palʋmmi a̱hli." Push ʋt achi tok. "Anato balilit kania la hinla, yohmi la hinla kʋt ithanali."

"Ʋno ahmako," Selena yʋt achi tok.

Ipokni yʋt nashuka nuktanla pisa mʋt yukpa tok. "Keyu, hash ayohma hekeyu. Ʋmmona ka̱, hash kanimapo hosh nana okpanit hash tahli na Issuba Ombinili Tʋshka yʋt hach ilbʋshala hinla ka̱ hash aiyohma hekeyu. Yʋmmʋt aia̱hli ka̱ ithanali."

7

Ipokni yʋt abinili faiohlichi okchamali awakaya tok. Tobi
hakshish micha ʋhli tʋptoa ashachi tukʋt tikba takali
apohlomichi tok. Onnaha tobi hoponachi kʋt asonak chito
alotua tok. "Selena maha isht ʋla," achi mʋt asonak chito pit
behliblit tok.

Push ʋt Issuba Ombinili Tʋshka isht anukfihinli tok. Kʋna
hʋt fama chi̱ keyukmʋt illi achi̱ hosh aionak mʋt, Chahta
kanimi kia hattak ʋpi humma hʋshi kanʋli iakaiya bʋnna tuk o̱
ahni tok. Anukfihinli tok . . . . .

Ipokni yʋt okhissa ont tiwit folota tok. Imanumpa hʋt
holisso apisa aiimma isht anukfohkachi tok. "Pehlichi apela
tikba ont ish falama moma hokma, ilʋppak fehna ho̱ -----ant
ish haiaka chi̱, mikmʋt chi famma mo̱machi̱h. Peh anumpuli
illa chi̱ keyu."

"Ithana li" Push ʋt lummasit achi tok. Chishba, nittak
kanohmi ka̱ aboha anu̱ka anta li tukmʋt amahleka hekeyu,
ili̱miha tok. Yʋmmʋt ikachukma hinla. Yohmi kia imihaksi tuk
osh himakma salaha cha falamʋt Ipokni inchukka ʋla kano
iklauecho ka hinla.

8

Push and Indian Time

Serena started to run to the front porch when she and Push reached their gate. Push pulled her back. "No, you don't!" he muttered. His brown face was getting red. His black eyes had sparks in them.

Serena stared at him. "Gee, Push, you look mean. I just wanted to...."

"I know. You wanted to tell Grandmother. I did it. I'm going to tell her."

Serena still stared at him. He looked so fierce. She couldn't believe he was her little brother, just six, two whole years younger than she was. "Okay," she said. "But I'm going to count to ten. If you haven't started I'm going to tell her."

Grandmother was on her front porch in her green rocker,

stringing beans. Push wished they could talk about the beans.

He liked to take a handful and eat them while they were raw

and crisp. But Grandmother didn't even look at the beans.

Her brown hands kept pulling off strings and snapping while

she looked right at him.

"You're late, children," she said.

Push tried to look up from the floor. His eye got as far as her

hands and her apron. Then he heard Serena, "one, two,

three...."

He gritted his teeth, and looked straight into Grandmother's eyes. All in one breath he said. "I had to go to the principal."

"I see," Grandmother said. Her hands kept working, but her face was waiting for him to go on.

"I---was late after recess. Three days—three afternoons in a row."

"Speak up, Push, don't look at the floor," she said.

"Well—the first day, I was fighting with Jimmy. Not mad fighting. He's my best friend. We just couldn't stop."

"What did Miss Sims say?" Of course, Serena had to butt in.

"She talked to both of us," he said.

"And the next time?" Grandmother asked.

"Well, the next time, yesterday, I almost went in with the others. But I saw a truck drive up. It was red, and the biggest truck I ever saw. I had to go look."

"So you were late again," Serena almost yelled the words.

He wanted to kick her. But he was already in enough trouble. And Grandmother's face was waiting.

11

"Miss Sims talked longer yesterday. Just to me."

Grandmother sighed. "But I guess you didn't hear her. Or you can't understand English."

Push squirmed. His face was burning. He wished his mother and dad would come home from work. He wished the wind would blow him off the porch.

At last he said, "I heard, but I forgot. Today when Cecil Gray got my whistle...."

"Gee Push, he's big. He's a fifth grader," Serena said.

"He's bigger than me. But I can run faster. I grabbed my whistle and I ran. I ran and ran. I ran so far I was—late again.

After a long time Grandmother said, "So Miss Sims took you to the principal?"

"No, she didn't take me. She sent me. After school."

"Was Mr. Graham mean?" Serena asked excitedly. "Did you get a licking?"

Push clenched his fists. When this was over—if it was ever over—he was going to scare the daylights out of Serena. All he could do now was say, "No, he wasn't mean. And I didn't get a licking."

"He just talked. He said we all had to be where we were suppose to be. So the teachers and everybody would know we weren't lost or anything."

Grandmother almost smiled. "Did he ask if you went by Indian-time?"

"What's that?" Push and Serena asked at the same time. "Well, at one time, the Choctaws—all Indians—would do things as the time was right for them to be done. A person spoke when he was ready to say his message; he wouldn't break in on another's time."

"Berries were picked when they were ripe—not too soon or too late. Today, if the berries aren't ripe, we import ripe ones. We can have them out of season. And now, we don't do things when it's time to do them, but we go by what the clock says."

Grandmother drew Push to her and held his hand. "The change isn't all bad. What if Miss Simms forgot to go by the bell? What if she kept you until she was ready to let you go home? I expect you at 3:30, and if you aren't here I would be afraid something bad had happened to you."

"To this day all Indians have a joke about themselves being late. When another Indian is late, someone is sure to ask, Is he going by Indian-time?"

"Like Push?" Serena asked.

"Not like Push is going to be from now on. That's for sure. Indian-time won't work anymore." Then she looked Push over from his scuffed brown loafers to his tousled black hair. "I'm kinda proud of Push."

"Proud of him?" Serena squeaked like she always did when she got mad. "Why if I had to go to the principal..."

"Hush, Serena. I'm certainly not proud of what he did. But I'm glad he went to Mr. Graham's office all by himself."

"I—I almost didn't." Push had to tell her. "I got to his door three times and ran outside. Then I went back. I stood there. Then I knocked."

"But you went," Grandmother reminded him. "So you're a real Choctaw."

"Why?" Push beat Serena to the question.

"Because when the Choctaw were running their own country, everyone always showed up—all alone—when he had to be punished for doing something wrong. No matter how bad the punishment. Whippings if they did something like steal cattle. If they killed someone they had to be shot."

"Didn't policemen put them in jail?" Push asked.

"There were no jails. And no policemen. There were Light Horsemen riding over the nation and keeping down trouble. I remember them."

Push and Serena were quiet, waiting to hear more.

"They put a red mark on a man's chest to show where the bullet would hit when he came back to be shot. Sometimes, he put the red mark on his own chest."

"That's—that's terrible," Push said. "I'd run away I know I would."

"Me too," Serena said.

Grandmother looked at their solemn faces and smiled. "No you wouldn't. First of all, neither one of you would ever do anything so bad that a Light Horseman would have to punish you. I'm sure of that."

Grandmother got up from the green rocker. She folded the pile of bean strings and snapped-off ends in her apron. "Bring the pan, Serena," She said as she pointed to the big kettle filled with beans she would cook tomorrow.

Push kept thinking about the Light Horsemen. He wondered if any of the Choctaws wanted to use Indian-time when they showed up to be whipped or killed. He wondered...

Grandmother turned as she opened the door. Her voice made him remember about school. "Another trip to the principal, Push, and you'll show up—right here—for more punishment. It won't be just talking."

"I know," Push whispered. Maybe it would be safer to stay in at recess for a few days, he told himself. That would be bad. But not so bad as coming home to Grandmother if he forgot and was late again.

Author
Mary M. Frye

Mary M. Frye loved children, especially Indian children. She loved to tell them stories. Some of her stories were written down and published. <u>Children's Activities</u> published one about a Cherokee girl (her daughter, Nancy) visiting the cabin of Sequoyah, who developed the Cherokee alphabet.

Born in 1903 in Bonham, Texas, Mary lived and went to school in Durant, Oklahoma, until the eighth grade. Then she attended Hollins College, a prep school and college in Roanoke, Virginia, through her junior year. Mary transferred to Oklahoma University and earned her bachelor and master's degrees in journalism.

She married Pliney Frye, a full-blood Cherokee attorney, and they lived in Wewoka, Oklahoma, where he practiced law. Their two children, Nancy and Jim, grew up with many friends among the Seminole-Creek children. She was a true storyteller and continued to tell and write stories about her children and their friends.

She moved back to Durant after her husband's death. She taught Latin and initiated and developed the journalism department at Southeastern Oklahoma State University (SOSU). She was an assistant professor.

In 1970 SOSU developed the Choctaw Bi-Lingual Education Program, a plan to provide a greater learning opportunities for Choctaw children in McCurtain County. It was through that program she wrote these charming stories of Choctaw children – Push, Serena, and Grandmother.

Illustrator
Norma Howard

Norma Howard is a Choctaw from Haskell County. Her paintings portray Choctaw life through her memories and her family. Her grandmother and her seven brothers and sisters are frequently featured in her artwork. She has won many awards for her paintings including first place at the Sante Fe Indian Market in 1997. She was selected as the featured artist for the Greenwood Cultural Center's 14th Annual Indian Art Festival. Only the top quality American Indian artists from across the United States are invited to display and sell their creations.

Translator
Henry Willis

Henry Willis was born in McClain County, Oklahoma, to Choctaw-speaking parents. As were most Indian children of his generation, he was sent to one of the boarding schools, Goodland Indian Orphanage, where he lived from age seven to nineteen. Unlike many children, Mr. Willis was able to return home on occasion, and thus was able to retain his Choctaw language. Mr. Willis was trained in electricity and electronics and spent much of his working career in radio and television broadcast engineering. After retirement in 1992, he began to devote himself to the study of the Choctaw language. He has been a language teacher at the University of Oklahoma and in church classes. He is a language consultant to the Choctaw Nation and to the University of Oklahoma and has participated in the curricula of Choctaw telecourses and Internet language courses. He has assisted in the production of Choctaw Nation language workbooks and audiotapes. He is a member of the Dictionary Project of the Choctaw Nation Language Program. He is the co-author of a Choctaw textbook, *Choctaw Language and Culture*, published by the University of Oklahoma Press. Mr. Willis lives in Moore, Oklahoma, with his wife Carole. They have seven children and many grandchildrenand devote themselves to many Indian educational and cultural activities.

By Virginia Espinoza,
Language Instructor
Choctaw Nation of Oklahoma

The Choctaw Light Horsemen

During the 1800's, officers, later known as the Light Horsemen, were established in Mississippi. Exclusively, the Choctaw Chief appointed these men. Provisions were made for this special unit at the signing of the Treaty of Doaks Stand.

The name "Lighthorse" actually came from the Cherokee. The name "Lighthorse" came from the Revolutionary War hero, General Henry Lee who was called "Lighthorse Harry" because of the quickness of his cavalry movements during conflicts. General Henry Lee was the father of Robert E. Lee.

The Choctaw Light Horsemen were what their name indicates. They were a hard riding, straight shooting, hard fighting body of men, who carried no excess equipment such as the militiamen carried. The Choctaw Light Horsemen's regular equipment consisted of a horse, saddle, rifle and revolver, while a few hands full of parched corn and some beef jerky in their pockets or saddlebags was the ration the Light Horsemen subsisted on while they moved swiftly from place to place.

In 1830, when the removal began, the Choctaw Light Horsemen also came continuing to serve in the capacity of officers in keeping order and peace in the new country. After the move to the West, the Choctaw Chief had nine Light Horsemen under his command. They served as his special agents, carrying messages, making arrests, keeping liquor at a distance during the council sessions, and assisting the U.S. Indian agent in the enforcement of laws. A law passed in 1888, required two Light Horsemen to be appointed to serve as bodyguards for the National Treasurer for the Choctaw people.

The Choctaw Light Horsemen's headquarters were at Tuskahoma and Atoka. These officers did not have any jurisdictional rights over the non-Indians or black men who were not citizens of their nations. What the Light Horsemen did on many occasions was to stop non-citizens from breaking the law in the Choctaw country. They arrested criminals and would detain them by turning them over to Deputy U.S. Marshals. The Choctaw Light Horsemen would on occasion assist the U.S. Marshals, removing illegal squatters and intruders who had been reported by the Choctaw Chief to the U.S. Indian agents. They arrested fugitives from justice turning them over to the officers of neighboring states when the governors made a request. However, their number one duty was upholding Federal laws in response to liquor sales in the Indian Territory.

These officers received a salary from the U.S. Government ranging from five to fifteen dollars a month. They also received additional monies from the tribe for removing intruders and for special services.

The Choctaw Light Horsemen were intensely loyal to the Choctaw people and their Chief. They were quick to respond to the need in the Choctaw country. Today, men of this caliber still exist and continue to serve the Choctaw people and their Chief. The Choctaw Chief Gregory E. Pyle has appointed Fred Bobb current Light Horseman. Fred Bobb serves as Sergeant-in-Arms during the judicial hearings.

By Hannah Bryan
Lanuguage Instructor
Choctaw Nation of Oklahoma

Glossary

1. **Balilit ishtia** – started to run

2. **Tobi hakshish** – stringing beans

3. **Holisso apisa** – school

4. **Pehlichi apela** – principle

5. **Ittibi** – fighting

6. **Fami** – licking (to whip, spank)

7. **Okpulo** – mean (ness)

8. **Nana kanihchi** – to punish

9. **H𝜈shi kan𝜈lli** – time

10. **Nan𝜈lhtoka** – policeman

11. **Ahchiba** – to be late

12. **Imapishia** – gate

13. **Abinili faiohliche okchamli** – green rocking chair

14. **Okchanki** – crisp

15. **Nafohka tikba takali** – apron

16. **Aboha K𝜈llo** – jail

17. **Issuba Ombinili T𝜈shka** – Light Horsemen